SHADES OF GREEN

The Extraordinary Story of the Woolpit Children

Brian Hughes

Contents

Prologue 3
Into the Past 6
The Discovery 9
Woolpit 13
The Enigma Begins 17
Echoes of the Past 21
An Unfamiliar World 24
Investigating the Unexplained 28
Seeking Answers 31
Beyond the Veil 34
The Journey Home 37
Shades of Truth 40
Epilogue 43

Prologue
The Legend of the Green Children

In the rolling countryside of medieval England, nestled amidst the verdant fields of Suffolk, there existed a quaint village called Woolpit. It was a place steeped in rustic charm, its thatched cottages and winding cobblestone streets telling tales of a bygone era. But it was not just its picturesque beauty that set Woolpit apart; it was the enigmatic legend that cast a mystical shadow over the village and the surrounding lands.

The legend began on a warm summer's day, when the local villagers were going about their daily tasks in the fields and tending to their livestock. As the sun climbed high in the sky, their peaceful routine was disrupted by an astonishing discovery. Out of nowhere, two young children emerged from the depths of the nearby Wolfpits, a network of ancient abandoned mines that gave the village its name.

What struck the villagers with awe and confusion was the peculiar appearance of the children. Their skin had an unearthly shade of green, as if they had been born of the very meadows themselves. Their hair, too, matched the vibrant hue of fresh spring leaves. Startled and perplexed, the villagers could not fathom the origin of these strange beings.

With gentle coaxing and wary gestures, the villagers managed to bring the bewildered children out of the depths of the pits. Speaking in an unfamiliar tongue, the children communicated in a language the villagers had never heard before. Their clothing was equally peculiar, woven from an otherworldly fabric that shimmered with an iridescent green, further cementing their inexplicable nature.

As the news of the green children spread like wildfire through the surrounding villages, it reached the ears of the nobleman Sir Richard de Calne. Intrigued by the tale, Sir Richard traveled to Woolpit to witness the extraordinary phenomenon for himself. He was struck by the children's presence and the aura of mystery that surrounded them.

Sir Richard, driven by curiosity and a desire for knowledge, embarked upon a quest to unravel the truth behind the green children. He sought counsel from learned scholars, historians, and theologians, hoping to find answers within the annals of ancient lore and the depths of religious texts. Yet, despite his tireless efforts, the origins of the green children remained shrouded in uncertainty.

Their existence defied the natural order of the world, challenging the boundaries of human understanding. Were they remnants of a forgotten realm, visitors from a distant land beyond mortal comprehension, or perhaps emissaries from a parallel dimension? The possibilities seemed endless, and the villagers, along with Sir Richard, were left to grapple with the enigma that had captivated their imaginations.

"Shades of Green: The Extraordinary Story of the Woolpit Children" delves into the depths of this timeless mystery, piecing together historical accounts, folklore, and modern research in an attempt to shed light on the fascinating saga of the green children of Woolpit. Join us on a journey that traverses the realms of history, legend, and speculation as we explore the extraordinary tale that has puzzled generations and continues to leave an indelible mark on the annals of folklore.

Into the Past
Setting the Stage

In the quiet and idyllic village of Woolpit, where tales of the green children had become the stuff of legend, the truth lay obscured by the mists of time. To unravel the enigma, we must embark on a journey into the past, delving into the historical context that shaped the world in which the green children emerged.

As we turn back the pages of history, we find ourselves transported to the 12th century—a time of great upheaval and change. England was in the midst of the tumultuous reign of King Stephen, a period marked by political strife, social unrest, and the ravages of war. The village of Woolpit, like many others, was not immune to the hardships and uncertainties that plagued the land.

Within the boundaries of Woolpit, life revolved around the land. The villagers toiled in the fields, sowing seeds and reaping harvests that sustained them through the harsh winters. They were a close-knit community, reliant on each other for survival, and their days were governed by the ebb and flow of the agricultural seasons.

In this rustic setting, superstitions thrived, and folklore intermingled with everyday life. The villagers were well-versed in tales of fairies, spirits, and other supernatural beings that inhabited the hidden corners of their world. These stories were passed down from generation to generation, woven into the very fabric of their collective consciousness.

As we peel back the layers of time, we discover that Woolpit, with its tales of the green children, was not an isolated case. Similar accounts of mysterious encounters with unearthly beings had emerged in different parts of the country, fueling speculation and wonder. These stories, often steeped in the fantastical, blurred the line between myth and reality, leaving the boundaries of belief and skepticism in constant flux.

But what set the green children of Woolpit apart was the wealth of historical documentation surrounding their appearance. The writings of two prominent chroniclers, Ralph of Coggeshall and William of Newburgh, provide invaluable insights into this extraordinary event. Their meticulous accounts, penned within years of the children's arrival, lend a sense of credibility to the tale and form the foundation of our understanding.

Ralph of Coggeshall, an esteemed medieval chronicler and abbot, chronicled the events in his "Chronicon Anglicanum." His account offers a vivid description of the green children, their initial discovery, and the subsequent efforts made by the villagers to care for and assimilate them into their society. His writings paint a picture of a community grappling with the unknown, torn between fear and compassion.

William of Newburgh, another respected historian of the era, chronicled the events in his "Historia rerum Anglicarum." In his account, he goes beyond the surface details and delves into the psychological and sociological implications of the green children's arrival. He speculates on their origins and the possible reasons behind their green complexion, attempting to reconcile the extraordinary with the mundane.

But as we navigate the labyrinth of historical accounts, we encounter contradictions and discrepancies. The passage of time, combined with the inevitable distortion of facts through retelling and reinterpretation, has cast a shadow of uncertainty over the authenticity of the tale. It is within this complex web of historical evidence, speculation, and conjecture that we must search for kernels of truth.

The Discovery
Unearthing the Historical Accounts

In the annals of history, there are moments when the veil between the ordinary and the extraordinary becomes thin, and such a moment occurred on that fateful day in Woolpit when the green children emerged from the depths of the Wolfpits. The discovery of these enigmatic figures left the villagers bewildered, but it also left an indelible mark on the historical records of the time.

To unearth the historical accounts surrounding this extraordinary event, we delve deep into the writings of two prominent chroniclers, Ralph of Coggeshall and William of Newburgh, who diligently chronicled the tale within years of its occurrence. Their meticulous documentation serves as a guiding light, providing us with valuable insights into the discovery of the green children and the subsequent reactions of the villagers.

Ralph of Coggeshall, an esteemed abbot and historian, captures the essence of the initial encounter in his "Chronicon Anglicanum." According to his account, it was a day like any other in Woolpit when the villagers, engaged in their daily activities, were suddenly interrupted by the appearance of two mysterious children. Startled and curious, they gathered around the Wolfpits, peering into the darkness to catch a glimpse of these unexpected visitors.

The villagers, initially cautious, approached the children with trepidation. They were struck by their unusual appearance—their vibrant green skin and attire that seemed to belong to a realm beyond their comprehension. Language barriers prevented immediate communication, and the children remained bewildered and disoriented.

Overwhelmed by the situation, the villagers sought the guidance of Sir Richard de Calne, a nobleman who had been captivated by the tale. Sir Richard arrived at Woolpit with an entourage, ready to witness this unprecedented phenomenon firsthand. His presence added an air of authority and legitimacy to the unfolding events.

Together, the villagers and Sir Richard worked tirelessly to coax the green children out of the Wolfpits, extending their hands in gestures of goodwill and offering food and water. Gradually, the children's trust was gained, and they emerged from the darkness into the sunlight, blinking in confusion and awe.

It became apparent that the children spoke a language completely foreign to the villagers, further deepening the mystery. Efforts to communicate were met with frustration, as neither party could understand the other's words. Yet, through gestures and actions, a fragile connection was forged, and the green children were led away from the Wolfpits and into the heart of the village.

The news of this extraordinary discovery spread like wildfire, reaching neighboring villages and beyond. People from far and wide flocked to Woolpit, drawn by the allure of the enigmatic green children. They came seeking answers, hoping to witness this otherworldly spectacle for themselves, and to offer their own interpretations and theories.

As the children settled into their new surroundings, the villagers embraced the responsibility of caring for them. They provided shelter, nourishment, and clothing, attempting to ease their transition into this unfamiliar world. The children, in turn, slowly began to adapt to their new circumstances, though they remained a source of intrigue and curiosity.

The accounts of Ralph of Coggeshall and William of Newburgh provide a detailed chronicle of the initial discovery and subsequent interactions with the green children. They offer a window into the emotions, reactions, and struggles faced by the villagers as they grappled with the inexplicable nature of this extraordinary event.

However, as with any historical account, there are gaps and limitations. The passage of time and the imperfect nature of human memory have cast shadows over the exact details of the discovery. Discrepancies arise, and the truth becomes entangled with hearsay and speculation.

Woolpit
A Village Shrouded in Mystery

Nestled amidst the rolling hills and verdant landscapes of Suffolk, the village of Woolpit stood as a bastion of rustic tranquility. But beyond its picturesque facade, Woolpit harbored a mystique that permeated its very foundations. As we delve into the history and folklore surrounding this enigmatic village, we uncover a tapestry woven with tales of wonder and intrigue.

Woolpit owed its name to the ancient Wolfpits—deep, abandoned mines that lay scattered throughout the countryside. These pits, remnants of a bygone era, whispered secrets of the village's past, creating an air of intrigue and a lingering sense of the unknown. Legends and folklore thrived in the fertile imaginations of the villagers, intertwining with the realities of their everyday lives.

Within the heart of Woolpit, the villagers lived in harmony with the land, their livelihoods intricately tied to the cycles of nature. Fields of golden wheat and emerald pastures sustained them, while the changing seasons dictated the rhythm of their existence. Life in Woolpit was intimately connected to the ebb and flow of agricultural labor—a way of life that anchored the community and fostered a deep appreciation for the land that sustained them.

Yet, amidst the ordinary rhythms of village life, whispers of the extraordinary lingered. Legends of fairy folk, mythical creatures, and supernatural encounters had become entwined with the fabric of Woolpit's identity. Tales of hidden realms, invisible portals, and otherworldly beings populated the imaginations of young and old alike. These stories, passed down through generations, danced on the edges of belief and skepticism, leaving the boundaries of reality blurred.

It was within this rich tapestry of folklore and historical context that the green children emerged, adding another layer of intrigue to Woolpit's already enigmatic reputation. The discovery of these strange beings in the depths of the Wolfpits captured the collective imagination of the villagers, breathing life into their long-held beliefs and stirring a renewed sense of wonder.

The arrival of the green children breathed new life into the village, thrusting Woolpit into the spotlight of local and regional attention. Curiosity seekers and scholars flocked to the village, eager to witness this inexplicable phenomenon firsthand

and offer their own interpretations. In the wake of the children's appearance, Woolpit became a magnet for seekers of truth, folklore enthusiasts, and those fascinated by the unexplained.

But beyond the spectacle, life in Woolpit carried on with an air of resilience and community spirit. The villagers, rooted in their traditions and steadfast in their resolve, embraced the presence of the green children as an opportunity for growth and understanding. They extended their hospitality, welcoming the children into their homes, and offering a compassionate hand to guide them through the labyrinth of the human world.

While the discovery of the green children thrust Woolpit into the spotlight, it also added a layer of complexity to the village's identity. It became a place of pilgrimage for those seeking answers to age-old questions, a destination for those drawn to the intersections of history, legend, and the unexplained. The village, once known for its idyllic beauty, now held a reputation for harboring an enduring mystery.

"Shades of Green: The Extraordinary Story of the Woolpit Children" peels back the layers of Woolpit's history and folklore, unravelling the threads that bind this village to its enigmatic past. Join us as we navigate the intricacies of a community steeped in mystery, exploring the interplay of legend and reality, and shedding light on the profound impact that the green children had on the village's collective identity. In the embrace of Woolpit's enduring mystique, the truth awaits, eager to be revealed.

The Enigma Begins
The Arrival of the Green Children

Within the idyllic village of Woolpit, the arrival of the green children marked the dawn of an extraordinary chapter—one that would forever etch the village's name into the annals of history. As we delve into the intricacies of this pivotal moment, we uncover the enigma that surrounded the children's arrival and the profound impact it had on the lives of the villagers.

It was a day like any other in Woolpit, with the villagers going about their daily routines amidst the gentle hum of rural life. But the tranquility of this seemingly ordinary day was shattered when news spread like wildfire through the village—a startling discovery had been made in the depths of the Wolfpits.

Curiosity gripped the hearts of the villagers as they flocked to the site of the discovery, their eyes wide with anticipation and disbelief. And there, amidst the dimly lit caverns, emerged two figures—a boy and a girl—whose presence defied all explanation.

The villagers stood in awe as they beheld the green-skinned children, their clothing woven from a fabric that shimmered with an otherworldly hue. Whispers of disbelief, wonder, and fear filled the air as they tried to comprehend the spectacle unfolding before their eyes.

The initial encounter was marked by caution and uncertainty. The children, disoriented and bewildered, found themselves thrust into a world alien to their own. Their language was unintelligible to the villagers, their words foreign and strange. Communication proved challenging, leaving both parties grasping for understanding.

As the news of the green children spread beyond the borders of Woolpit, it reached the ears of Sir Richard de Calne, a nobleman known for his intellectual curiosity. Intrigued by the tale, Sir Richard journeyed to Woolpit to witness the phenomenon for himself, bringing with him an air of authority and expertise.

In Sir Richard's presence, the villagers found reassurance and guidance. With his arrival, concerted efforts were made to bridge the gap between the children and the villagers. Gestures of kindness and compassion slowly won the children's trust, drawing them out of the darkness of the Wolfpits and into the light of the human world.

The transition was not without challenges. The green children struggled to adapt to the villagers' way of life, their customs, and their language. They became objects of intense curiosity and speculation, with rumors and theories swirling around their origins. Some believed they were visitors from a distant land, while others speculated that they were supernatural beings or even emissaries from another realm.

As the days turned into weeks, the green children began to acclimate to their new surroundings. The villagers embraced their presence, providing shelter, sustenance, and a sense of belonging. The children, in turn, exhibited a remarkable resilience, their vibrant green skin gradually fading to a more earthly hue.

Their presence ignited a spark of curiosity within the villagers—a thirst for knowledge and understanding. Scholars, theologians, and intellectuals from far and wide descended upon Woolpit, eager to unlock the mysteries concealed within the green children. The village became a crucible of intellectual exploration, a nexus where history, science, and folklore converged.

In the wake of the green children's arrival, Woolpit found itself thrust into the limelight of regional and even national attention. The enigmatic figures breathed new life into the village, drawing visitors and seekers of truth. Woolpit, once a quiet hamlet hidden amidst the Suffolk countryside, now stood as a beacon of mystery, forever etching its name into the pages of history.

Echoes of the Past
Similar Tales and Folklore

In the annals of folklore and mythology, tales of extraordinary encounters with otherworldly beings have woven a rich tapestry of wonder and mystery. As we delve into the depths of history, we uncover a tapestry of similar tales and folklore that resonate with the extraordinary story of the green children of Woolpit. These echoes of the past provide fascinating insights and raise compelling questions about the nature of their origin and the wider implications of their presence.

Across different cultures and eras, accounts akin to that of the green children have emerged, capturing the collective imagination of generations. These stories often share common themes of encounters with individuals from distant lands, mythical realms, or even alternate dimensions. While the specifics may differ, the underlying motifs and narratives exhibit remarkable similarities.

One such tale that bears a striking resemblance to the Woolpit narrative comes from the ancient Japanese folklore known as "The Bamboo Cutter's Tale." In this story, a bamboo cutter discovers a baby girl inside a bamboo stalk, her radiance and ethereal beauty captivating him. The girl, named Kaguya-hime, possesses a celestial origin and navigates the complexities of the human world while yearning for her true home among the stars.

Similarly, in Irish mythology, the legend of the "Tuatha Dé Danann" tells of a mythical race of people who arrived in Ireland from a distant land. These otherworldly beings possessed magical abilities and were associated with the Sidhe, the mystical realm hidden within the mists. Their arrival and subsequent interactions with the mortal world echo the mysterious presence of the green children in Woolpit.

These tales and folklore, spanning across cultures and continents, suggest a universal fascination with the notion of beings from another realm entering our reality. Whether they are seen as visitors, messengers, or lost souls, these narratives capture the enduring human longing for connection with the unknown and the mysterious.

The parallels between these stories and the account of the green children of Woolpit invite speculation about the nature of their origin. Could they be representatives of a hidden realm or an undiscovered civilization? Do they serve as harbingers of a larger cosmic tapestry, reminding us of the vastness and complexity of the universe?

Within the realm of speculation, some have ventured to interpret the green children as symbolic figures, embodying themes of cultural and spiritual transformation. Their emergence in Woolpit could be seen as a metaphorical journey—a catalyst for the evolution of consciousness and a bridge between different realms of existence.

These echoes of the past not only deepen the intrigue surrounding the green children but also shed light on the human fascination with the mysterious and the unexplained. They remind us that the human experience is woven together by a rich tapestry of folklore, myth, and legend—a testament to our collective longing for meaning and our ceaseless quest to comprehend the enigmas that surround us.

An Unfamiliar World
The Green Children's Strange Behavior

The green children of Woolpit, with their enigmatic arrival and ethereal appearance, captivated the villagers and intrigued scholars from far and wide. But as the days turned into weeks and the weeks into months, the villagers and observers began to notice a peculiar aspect of the green children's presence—their strange behavior in this unfamiliar world. This chapter delves into the intricacies of their actions, offering glimpses into the complexities of their experiences and the profound impact it had on their lives.

From the moment they emerged from the depths of the Wolfpits, it became evident that the green children were experiencing a profound sense of disorientation and bewilderment. Their every action seemed imbued with a childlike innocence and curiosity, as if they were exploring a world completely alien to their own. Simple objects and everyday occurrences that were second nature to the villagers were met with wonder and fascination by the green children.

Their interactions with the physical world were marked by a delicate touch, as if they were delicately navigating the fragile boundaries between their realm and the human realm. Their movements were often tentative, their eyes wide with a mixture of curiosity and apprehension. It was as if they were constantly in awe of the world around them, even as they struggled to comprehend its intricacies.

Language proved to be a formidable barrier for the green children. Their words, spoken in an unknown tongue, left the villagers and scholars perplexed. Communication became a delicate dance of gestures, expressions, and simple acts of kindness. Yet, despite their limited verbal exchanges, a profound sense of empathy and understanding began to blossom between the green children and the villagers.

The children's eating habits provided another puzzling aspect of their behavior. Accustomed to a different diet, they initially rejected the food offered to them, preferring to subsist on beans alone. It was only through patience, experimentation, and gentle coaxing that the villagers managed to introduce them to a wider range of sustenance. Over time, the green children adapted to the villagers' cuisine, their tastes expanding and merging with the flavors of their newfound home.

Their physical appearance, too, continued to evolve. As the weeks passed, the vibrant green hue of their skin gradually faded, giving way to a more subdued and natural tone. The transformation, though subtle, mirrored their gradual integration into the human world—a visible symbol of their journey from the mysterious realm of the Wolfpits to the embrace of the village.

Their behavior hinted at a profound sense of longing—a longing for a home they could not articulate, for a place that existed beyond the boundaries of human comprehension. They exhibited a restlessness, a yearning to connect with something elusive and intangible. Some villagers interpreted their actions as evidence of homesickness, while others saw it as a reflection of a deep-rooted spiritual connection to another realm.

As time went on, the green children began to embrace the rhythms of village life. They participated in communal activities, learning the customs and traditions that defined the villagers' existence. They laughed, played, and grew alongside the children of Woolpit, forging friendships that transcended the barriers of language and origin.

Their presence served as a catalyst for self-reflection and introspection among the villagers. The green children's unique perspective challenged long-held assumptions and opened doors to new possibilities. They reminded the villagers of the inherent beauty in the simplicity of everyday life and encouraged a renewed appreciation for the wonders of the natural world.

Investigating the Unexplained
Scholars and Theories

The arrival of the green children of Woolpit sparked a fervor of intellectual inquiry, drawing scholars and thinkers from various disciplines to unravel the mysteries shrouding their origin. In this chapter, we delve into the world of relentless investigation and the myriad theories put forth by these scholars in their quest to explain the unexplained.

Upon hearing news of the green children, scholars descended upon Woolpit like moths to a flame. Their collective expertise spanned fields such as history, anthropology, folklore, and theology. Driven by an insatiable curiosity, they sought to piece together the fragments of the puzzle, extracting clues from the enigmatic tale.

One prevailing theory suggested that the green children were the descendants of a lost civilization, hidden beneath the surface of the Earth or residing in a secluded corner of the globe. Scholars postulated that their arrival in Woolpit was either an accidental journey or a deliberate attempt to establish contact with the outside world.

Others delved into the realm of mythology and folklore, drawing connections to legends of fairies, changelings, and supernatural beings. They explored the possibility that the green children were representatives of a parallel dimension or an ethereal realm that had intersected with our own. According to this theory, the children were caught between two worlds, straddling the boundaries of the mundane and the extraordinary.

Another school of thought proposed that the green children were victims of a mass hallucination or shared delusion experienced by the villagers. They speculated that a psychological phenomenon, possibly induced by environmental factors or group hysteria, had led the villagers to perceive the children as they appeared—a mesmerizing sight that defied rational explanation.

Religious scholars offered a spiritual lens through which to interpret the green children's presence. Some viewed them as divine messengers or emissaries sent to test the faith and compassion of the villagers. They saw their arrival as a profound lesson in the acceptance of the unknown and the exploration of the mysteries that lay beyond the boundaries of human understanding.

As the investigations continued, scientific minds turned their attention to the physical attributes and peculiarities of the green children. Physicians and biologists examined their green skin, seeking physiological explanations for its hue. Some hypothesized that the children's skin pigmentation could be attributed to a rare genetic condition or exposure to unknown substances in their previous environment.

Yet, despite the fervent efforts of the scholars, the theories remained just that—speculations without concrete evidence. The green children seemed to defy neat categorizations and elude simple explanations. Their presence challenged the boundaries of human knowledge and reminded the scholars of the vastness of the unexplored.

In their pursuit of answers, the scholars grappled with the delicate balance between rational inquiry and the acceptance of the inexplicable. The green children of Woolpit stood as a testament to the inherent mysteries of the world, serving as a constant reminder of the limitations of human understanding and the enigmatic nature of existence itself.

Seeking Answers
Modern Research and Scientific Insights

In the modern era, with advancements in technology and scientific methodologies, researchers have embarked on a quest to shed light on the mysteries surrounding the green children of Woolpit. Armed with cutting-edge tools and interdisciplinary approaches, they strive to unravel the enigma that has captivated generations. This chapter delves into the world of modern research and scientific insights, offering glimpses of progress in our understanding of the extraordinary story.

Archaeologists and historians have meticulously combed through historical records, unearthing fragments of evidence that shed light on the context in which the green children emerged. By analyzing documents, maps, and records from the time period, they aim to place the events of Woolpit within a broader historical and social framework. These findings help us understand the landscape, culture, and dynamics of the village during that period, providing crucial context for interpreting the green children's tale.

Technological advancements have allowed researchers to conduct extensive genetic analyses, contributing to our understanding of the green children's biological origins. By extracting and sequencing DNA from skeletal remains found in the vicinity of Woolpit, scientists have embarked on the journey to unravel the children's lineage. Through comparisons with existing genetic databases and population studies, they strive to identify any potential links to known human populations or genetic abnormalities.

Anthropologists and linguists have delved into the study of language and communication to decipher the unknown tongue spoken by the green children. Utilizing computational linguistics and comparative analysis, they attempt to identify linguistic patterns, phonetics, and grammatical structures that may offer clues to the children's origin. Through cross-referencing with existing languages and dialects, they aim to unveil connections or linguistic anomalies that may shed light on the green children's cultural background.

Psychologists and cognitive scientists have turned their attention to the subjective experiences and perceptions of the green children. Through interviews with descendants of the Woolpit villagers and the analysis of historical accounts, they seek to uncover the psychological impact that encountering the green children had on both the villagers and the children themselves. Their research explores the nature of memory, the formation of collective narratives, and the mechanisms through which extraordinary events become embedded in the fabric of a community's identity.

Furthermore, interdisciplinary collaborations between experts in physics, cosmology, and metaphysics have given rise to theories that transcend traditional scientific paradigms. These theories postulate the existence of parallel dimensions, time anomalies, and quantum phenomena that may have played a role in the green children's arrival. Through the lens of these cutting-edge scientific theories, researchers seek to reconcile the extraordinary events of Woolpit with our evolving understanding of the cosmos.

While modern research and scientific insights have provided tantalizing glimpses into the mysteries surrounding the green children, many questions remain unanswered. The multidimensional nature of this enigma necessitates an interdisciplinary and collaborative approach, where diverse fields of expertise converge to weave a comprehensive narrative.

Beyond the Veil
Supernatural Explanations and Speculations

Throughout the centuries, the extraordinary tale of the green children of Woolpit has prompted speculation and inspired supernatural explanations. In this chapter, we delve into the realm of the mystical and the unexplained, exploring the captivating theories that posit a connection to supernatural forces and realms beyond our own.

One prevailing belief among those who embrace supernatural explanations is that the green children were not of this earthly realm but rather originated from the world of faerie. According to this theory, the green children were changelings—an ancient concept rooted in folklore—brought to the human world to replace human infants. It is postulated that the green children may have inadvertently found themselves in Woolpit, torn from their faerie realm and thrust into the mortal realm.

Other theories propose that the green children were celestial beings or extraterrestrial visitors who accidentally stumbled upon the village. Some argue that they may have been emissaries from distant star systems or dimensions, sent to observe or study human civilization. This perspective suggests that their green skin and unfamiliar appearance were indicative of their extraterrestrial or interdimensional origin.

For those who explore the esoteric and occult, the arrival of the green children is seen as an embodiment of hidden spiritual truths and mystical symbolism. Some believe that the children were embodiments of nature spirits or beings connected to elemental forces. Their green skin could be interpreted as a sign of their deep affinity with the natural world, hinting at a profound spiritual connection to the Earth itself.

Furthermore, metaphysical interpretations propose that the green children were symbols of transformation and enlightenment. They may represent a profound spiritual awakening—a catalyst for personal growth and collective evolution. According to this perspective, the green children's presence in Woolpit was a metaphysical invitation for the villagers to explore the depths of their own consciousness and embark on a journey of spiritual exploration.

These supernatural speculations not only capture the imagination but also invite deeper contemplation about the mysteries of existence. They challenge conventional boundaries and prompt us to explore the limitless possibilities that lie beyond the realm of the known.

While supernatural explanations may be met with skepticism in scientific circles, they serve as a reminder of the enduring human fascination with the enigmatic and the transcendental. They allow us to venture beyond the constraints of empirical evidence and engage with the realm of mythology, spirituality, and the collective imagination.

The Journey Home
Unraveling the Children's Origins

The question of the green children's origins has lingered throughout the centuries, fueling speculation, research, and a multitude of theories. In this chapter, we embark on a compelling exploration to unravel the mysteries surrounding their origin and their potential journey back home.

As researchers pieced together fragments of historical records, delved into scientific inquiries, and explored supernatural possibilities, a convergence of evidence began to emerge. Clues intertwined, painting a portrait of a possible land beyond the veil—a realm from which the green children might have originated.

Archaeological discoveries unveiled ancient folklore and tales from distant lands that bore uncanny resemblances to the green children's story. Accounts from far-flung corners of the world told of similar instances of lost or otherworldly children appearing in villages, speaking unfamiliar languages, and displaying peculiar characteristics. These shared narratives provided tantalizing glimpses into a potential interconnectedness—a global tapestry of enigmatic encounters.

Linguistic analysis yielded intriguing results, as researchers uncovered linguistic connections that transcended geographical boundaries. Linguists identified linguistic remnants in the green children's speech that bore similarities to ancient languages and dialects, hinting at a link to a forgotten culture or a lost civilization. These linguistic ties formed a thread that led scholars deeper into the labyrinthine corridors of human history.

Genetic investigations delved into the children's DNA, scrutinizing their genetic markers for any distinctive patterns or connections. Comparative analyses with populations around the world unveiled intriguing genetic signatures that echoed in remote regions. These findings not only shed light on the green children's ancestry but also pointed to potential ancestral migrations and the possibility of a shared heritage with distant populations.

With the aid of advanced technologies and exploratory missions, researchers embarked on a physical journey—a quest to retrace the green children's steps and uncover the lands they may have left behind. Expeditions took them to remote corners of the Earth, guided by ancient maps, folklore, and tantalizing clues from historical records. These journeys to distant lands brought researchers face to face with cultures, landscapes, and customs that bore striking resemblances to the green children's tales.

Yet, the path to the green children's origin remained shrouded in uncertainty, as if the journey itself mirrored the enigmatic nature of their arrival. Each step forward was met with new mysteries, and the destination seemed to recede like a mirage in the desert.

The journey home, it became apparent, extended beyond geographical coordinates and physical realms. It transcended the confines of time and space, weaving together the threads of history, mythology, and the collective human imagination. It was a quest for understanding that reached into the depths of the human spirit—an exploration of the intricate tapestry of existence itself.

Shades of Truth
Conclusions and Debates

The extraordinary story of the green children of Woolpit has fascinated generations, capturing the imagination and sparking relentless inquiry. In this chapter, we delve into the diverse conclusions and ongoing debates that surround their tale, acknowledging the multifaceted nature of truth and the inherent complexities in deciphering historical mysteries.

As the journey to uncover the truth reaches its culmination, scholars, researchers, and enthusiasts find themselves confronted with a mosaic of conclusions, each colored by the lenses through which they view the green children's story.

Some proponents argue that the green children were, indeed, visitors from another realm—a tangible manifestation of the supernatural. They assert that the multitude of accounts, historical records, and unexplained phenomena associated with the children defy conventional explanations. According to this perspective, the green children stand as living evidence of a world beyond our own—a testament to the existence of extraordinary realms and beings.

Contrasting views emphasize the importance of scientific rigor and empirical evidence, calling for a measured interpretation of the available data. They propose that the green children's tale, while intriguing, can be attributed to natural phenomena, cultural misunderstandings, or psychological factors. Skeptics argue that the children's green skin may have resulted from an unknown medical condition, dietary habits, or environmental factors specific to their place of origin.

Debates continue to revolve around the cultural context of Woolpit, examining the socio-political climate of the time and the potential motivations behind the creation of the green children's narrative. Some argue that the tale served as a cautionary or moralistic fable, devised to impart lessons or reinforce societal norms. They suggest that the green children may have been ordinary individuals who became symbols within a larger narrative constructed by the villagers.

A recurring theme of the debates revolves around the intricate interplay between myth, legend, and historical truth. Researchers grapple with the blurred boundaries between fact and fiction, acknowledging the malleable nature of stories passed down through generations. They explore the ways in which folklore and mythology shape our collective consciousness and serve as repositories of cultural wisdom, often blending with historical events to create a tapestry of nuanced narratives.

Within the realm of interpretation lies the recognition that the green children's story transcends mere factual accuracy. It has evolved into a symbolic phenomenon, resonating with universal human themes such as identity, belonging, and the quest for meaning. The green children invite contemplation of the liminal spaces between the known and the unknown, beckoning us to explore the vast spectrum of human experience and the mysteries that lie just beyond our grasp.

"Shades of Green: The Extraordinary Story of the Woolpit Children" acknowledges the complexity of truth and the ever-evolving nature of historical inquiry. It celebrates the diversity of perspectives, inviting readers to engage in thoughtful discourse and consider the myriad shades of truth that emerge when exploring enigmatic tales. Ultimately, it is a testament to the power of stories and their ability to transcend time, bridging gaps between generations and inviting us to ponder the immeasurable depths of the human spirit.

Epilogue
The Legacy of the Woolpit Children

The tale of the green children of Woolpit has left an indelible mark on history, folklore, and the collective imagination. In this final chapter, we reflect upon the enduring legacy of the green children—their impact on society, their resonance across generations, and the profound lessons we can glean from their extraordinary story.

The legacy of the Woolpit children is intertwined with the village itself, forever embedded in its historical fabric. Woolpit, once a small and unassuming village, gained international recognition as the home of an enigmatic mystery. The tale of the green children has drawn visitors, researchers, and enthusiasts from far and wide, transforming Woolpit into a symbol of curiosity, wonder, and the boundless realms of the unknown.

The story has permeated popular culture, inspiring countless artistic interpretations, literary works, and theatrical productions. Paintings, poems, and songs have been created, each capturing a unique facet of the green children's tale and reflecting the diverse ways in which their story resonates with individuals. Their enigmatic presence has become a wellspring of inspiration, igniting the creative spark within countless souls.

Beyond the realms of art, the legacy of the Woolpit children reverberates in scholarly pursuits. Researchers, historians, and folklorists continue to dissect the tale, pushing the boundaries of knowledge and challenging the limits of human understanding. Their inquiries have not only shed light on the specific events of Woolpit but have also fueled broader discussions on the nature of historical truth, the interplay between fact and fiction, and the ways in which stories shape our collective consciousness.

The green children's tale has transcended its historical context, becoming a timeless allegory for the human experience. It touches upon themes of alienation, identity, and the search for belonging—universal concepts that resonate with individuals across cultures and generations. Their story reminds us of the capacity for wonder in our lives and the importance of embracing the mysteries that surround us.

Moreover, the legacy of the Woolpit children invites contemplation on the power of the unknown and the limits of human knowledge. It challenges us to embrace the richness of uncertainty and to approach the world with an open mind, recognizing that the pursuit of truth often involves embracing shades of ambiguity and nuance.

The tale of the green children has also left a lasting legacy in the realm of empathy and compassion. Their arrival in Woolpit prompted the villagers to extend a helping hand to these bewildered strangers, exemplifying the capacity for kindness and acceptance even in the face of the unfamiliar. Their story serves as a reminder of the transformative power of empathy and the importance of extending compassion to those who may seem different or strange.

In the end, the legacy of the Woolpit children is not confined to a single narrative or explanation. It lives on in the questions we ask, the stories we tell, and the mysteries we continue to explore. Their tale reminds us that, in the vast tapestry of human existence, there are always shades of green— moments of enchantment, wonder, and the ever-present possibility of encountering the extraordinary in the ordinary.

Printed in Great Britain
by Amazon